W9-AJN-179

For Floyd.

Book design by Joyce Marie Kuchar.
The artwork in this book was rendered in Prismacolor pencils on black paper.

Printed in Hong Kong.

Library of Congress Cataloging-in-Publication Data
Bourke, Linda.
Eye Count: a book of counting puzzles / by Linda Bourke.
36p. 25.5 x 21.5 cm.
ISBN 0-8118-0732-0
1. Counting—Juvenile literature. [1. Counting. 2. Picture puzzles.]
I. Title.
QA113.B67 1995
793.7'4—dc20
[E] 94-45301
CIP
AC

Distributed in Canada by Raincoast Books
8680 Cambie Street, Vancouver, B.C. V6P 6M9

10 9 8 7 6 5 4 3 2 1

Chronicle Books
275 Fifth Street
San Francisco, California 94103

FOR McCULLOUGH
&
JACK

Linda Bourke

JUNE 95

Eye Count

A Book of Counting Puzzles

by Linda Bourke

CHRONICLE BOOKS • SAN FRANCISCO

1

one

2

two

3

three

4

four

5

five

6

six

7

seven

8

eight

9

nine

10

ten

11

eleven

12

twelve

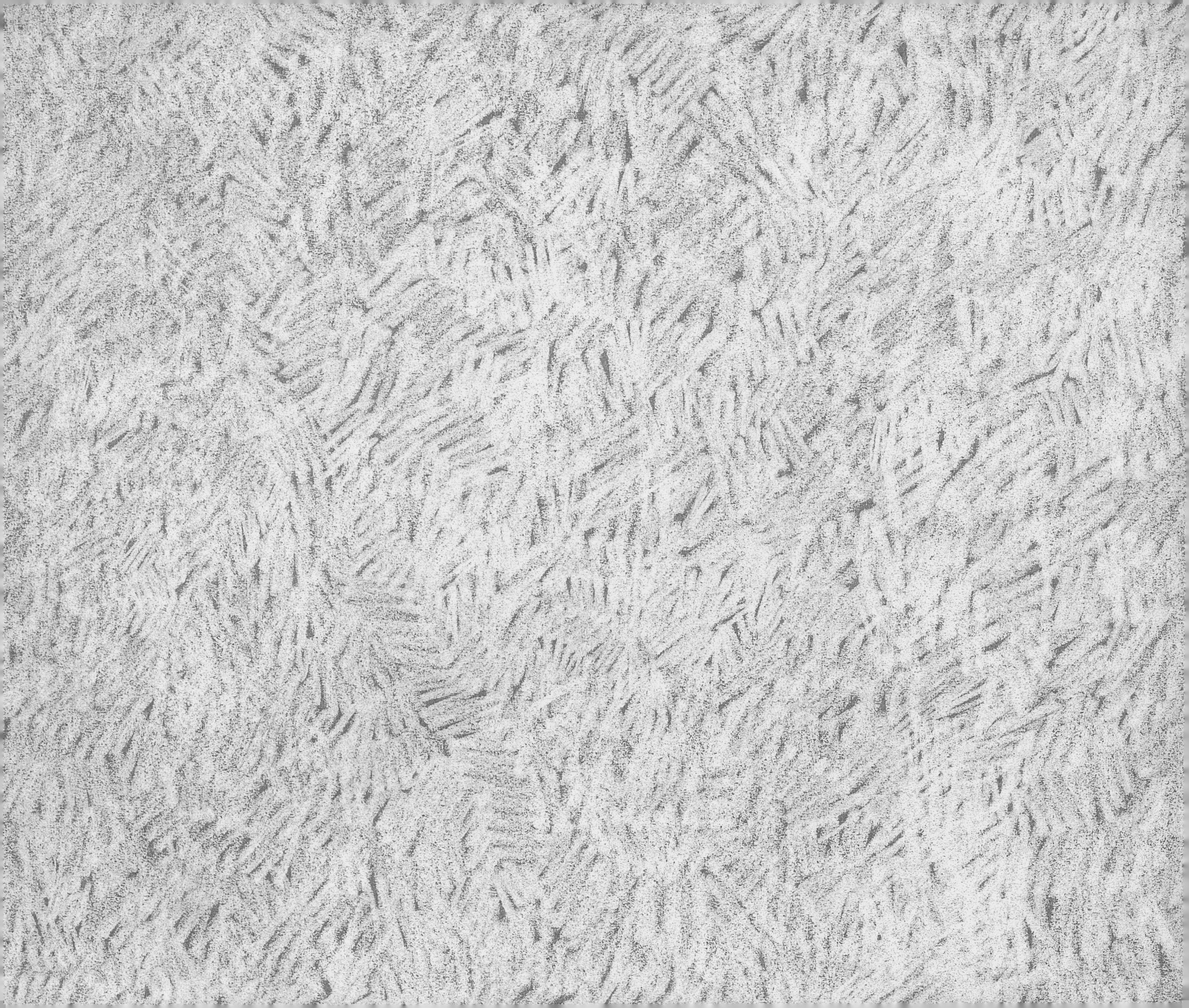